The Alden Family Mysteries
by Gertrude Chandler Warner

THE BOXCAR CHILDREN
SURPRISE ISLAND
THE YELLOW HOUSE MYSTERY
MYSTERY RANCH
MIKE'S MYSTERY
BLUE BAY MYSTERY
THE WOODSHED MYSTERY
THE LIGHTHOUSE MYSTERY
MOUNTAIN TOP MYSTERY
SCHOOLHOUSE MYSTERY
CABOOSE MYSTERY
HOUSEBOAT MYSTERY
SNOWBOUND MYSTERY
TREE HOUSE MYSTERY
BICYCLE MYSTERY
MYSTERY IN THE SAND
MYSTERY BEHIND THE WALL
BUS STATION MYSTERY
BENNY UNCOVERS A MYSTERY

Gertrude Chandler Warner

Tree House Mystery

Illustrations:
David Cunningham

ALBERT WHITMAN & Company   Chicago

O1018   9115

ISBN 0-8075-8086-4
L.C. Catalog Card 77-91744

12   11

Contents

CHAPTER 1

New Next Door

One afternoon in early July Benny Alden came in the front door and rushed down the hall to the stairs.

"Hey, Henry!" he shouted. "Jessie! Violet!"

"What's the matter, Ben?" said a quiet voice. Henry stood at the top of the stairs. He looked down at his younger brother. "What's all the fuss?"

"Somebody's moving in next door! Imagine having neighbors!" Benny went on. "I can't remember anyone ever living there. And that's odd, too, because the house is so near the beach."

"Grandfather always calls it the beach house," Violet said. "I always thought people used to spend summers there."

"Well, there's a family there now," Benny said. "There are two boys, only I wish they were a little older."

"My, that house has been empty so long," said Jessie Alden. She stood beside Henry at the top of the stairs. "Who are they, Ben?"

"I don't know," answered Benny. "They're strangers."

"Oh, what do they look like?" Violet asked.

"You can see for yourself. Go and look out of Grandfather's bedroom window."

Grandfather Alden had gone to work, so his room was empty.

Benny raced upstairs to Mr. Alden's room, and

Violet, Henry, and Jessie followed.

The next house was really not very near. The Alden place, after all, was quite big. There was a large lawn and a rose garden, and some woods between it and the house next door. That house, too, had many trees around it.

The Aldens could see a mover's truck in front of the house that had been empty. Four men were going into the house with furniture, and right by the truck stood a man and a woman and two boys.

Benny raised the screen and put his head out of the window.

"You can't make them hear you, Benny," said Jessie.

"Well, I'm going to try," replied Benny. "Yoo-hoo, welcome!" he shouted.

The strangers looked up. The boys began to smile and wave when they saw the four Aldens. The mother and father were not as quick to smile. Benny thought, "They act as if they don't want anyone to notice they are moving in."

While the boys waved the man called, "Thank you!" Then he did smile and began to walk toward the Alden house. The boys followed him. "Our name is Beach," he called. "We are going to be your new neighbors."

"That's good," answered Jessie. "That house has been empty too long."

Mr. Beach said, "This is Jeffrey, and this is Sammy. I'm sure they will like living here."

Jessie smiled at the boys. She said, "Hello, boys. You know, everyone calls your house the beach house. We thought it was because it was a summer place so near the beach. But it is your name, isn't it?"

"Yes, just the way your house is the Alden house," said Jeffrey. He was the older of the two boys.

"Oh, you know our name?" said Benny.

The boys looked at their father. Mr. Beach said, "Oh, everyone knows the Alden place."

The Aldens thought, "He acts as if he has known the Alden place for a long time. Maybe he isn't such a stranger after all."

Benny said, "I'll be over sometime when you get settled. Then we can get acquainted."

"Come any time," replied Mr. Beach, starting back. The Aldens noticed that Mrs. Beach had not said a word.

As the Beach family went into their new house, Violet said, "I have an idea."

The others looked at her because Violet's ideas were always good.

She said, "Mrs. Beach will be too tired to get supper, so let's send their supper over to them."

Nobody said a word. The Aldens looked at each other. Then they turned and went to the kitchen, all smiling.

Mrs. McGregor was the housekeeper and cook. She had been with the Aldens for many years and she loved them all. Now Mrs. McGregor was sitting in her big rocking chair in the kitchen, with her cat on her lap.

Jessie began, "Oh, Mrs. McGregor, we'd like to cook some supper for our new neighbors. The Beach family is moving in right now. There are four of them. Could we make a casserole?"

"Why not?" asked Mrs. McGregor, smiling. "I'll sit and watch you work."

That was what the Alden children liked best. They liked to work without any help, and Mrs. McGregor knew it well.

Everyone began to work. Benny opened cans of tomato soup. Henry peeled onions and cut them up. Violet got out some hamburger and began to break it up to cook in a pan. Jessie cooked macaroni and got out the cheese.

When all the things were cooked, Jessie put them together in a big dish and covered the top with cheese. She put it in the oven to bake.

Mrs. McGregor waited until Jessie had closed the oven door. Then she said, "Did you say a Beach family is moving in next door? I've been sitting here thinking about that old house. I haven't been in it for years."

"But you were in it once?" Benny asked.

"Yes," Mrs. McGregor said. "I must have been quite little because everything seemed huge to me. Let's see, I was invited there for a birthday party."

"That sounds like fun," Violet said. "Then there must have been a family with children there."

"No," Mrs. McGregor said. "That's the odd part about it. I'm sure this was special. An old lady lived there, I remember that. Even when I was little I thought it was sad that there was that great big house and just an old lady in it. Oh, I wish I could remember more."

The Aldens kept quiet while Mrs. McGregor rocked back and forth. At last she shook her head. "No, I can't remember anything else except that somebody got a little hunting horn. I remember a little boy with a great big sailor collar with ruffles. Maybe the horn was a birthday present."

"What happened to the old lady?" asked Jessie.

"I don't remember," Mrs. McGregor said. "My family moved out of town and we lived on a farm. Since your grandfather has been here, nobody has lived in the house. I know that much."

Benny said, "I guess the house always seemed a little spooky with all those big trees around it."

Jessie said, "Most of the time we don't think about the house being there at all. It's been empty so long."

"I like to think about two boys being there now," Benny said. "Can we take them some dessert?"

Mrs. McGregor said, "You can take four of my orange puddings. I made a dozen."

"Oh, thank you," said Violet. "That's wonderful."

So that was how the Beach family had their first supper as neighbors to the Alden family. It was true that Mrs. Beach was tired from moving and was glad to see a meal brought in by four smiling children.

A few days later Jessie was looking at the Greenfield News. "Here's something about our neighbors," she said.

"What is it?" asked Henry. "It seems funny that we have to find out about them by reading a newspaper."

Jessie read the news story aloud. It said that Mr.

and Mrs. John Beach had moved into the house next to that owned by Mr. James Henry Alden. It also told that Mr. Beach was a scientist for the new Greenfield Chemical Company.

"Let me see," Benny said. Then he sounded disappointed. "It doesn't say anything at all about two boys in the family. I guess they don't count."

"I think we had better go over and call on our new neighbors," Mr. Alden said.

Benny said, "We'd better go in the evening. The mother and father go out every day. I guess they work."

"You see a lot, Ben," Jessie told him. "You must spend a lot of time looking out the window."

"No," Benny said. "I just happened to see the Beaches get in their car and drive off in the morning. Then I happened to see them when they came home in the afternoon."

Grandfather and the others laughed at Benny. They walked over to the house next door and rang the bell.

Mr. Beach came to the door and asked the Aldens to come in. The Beaches were all at home.

Mr. Beach was a tall thin man with very dark eyes and brown hair. He went back and sat down at his desk. He took off his glasses and said, "You were kind to cook that supper for us. My wife was very tired from moving."

Mrs. Beach said, "How do you do, Mr. Alden? Yes, I was tired. I didn't enjoy moving."

"The boys loved the casserole," Mr. Beach said suddenly. "They like all kinds of spaghetti and macaroni. They liked the dessert, too. And so did I."

Mrs. Beach said nothing else, and the two boys did not say a single word.

Mr. Beach was shy and uneasy, and Mrs. Beach acted as if she were thinking of something else. Even Benny found it hard to talk to the new neighbors. Nobody seemed interested in what he had to say.

"We really have a big dog," said Benny. "His name is Watch, but he isn't here this summer. My Aunt Jane wanted him on the farm."

Nobody said a word. They just looked at him.

Poor Benny. He tried again. "You'd like our dog. He's a nice, gentle dog."

Mr. and Mrs. Beach just nodded politely.

At last the Aldens went home. "They aren't very friendly," said Jessie, as they opened their own door.

"I agree with Jessie," said Benny.

After that, nothing happened. Nothing at all.

One day Benny said, "I'd never know we had any neighbors. They certainly aren't friendly. We asked them to come and see us, but they didn't even say they would. And they haven't."

Even Grandfather Alden said, "It seems strange to me, too, Benny. We don't want to bother them if they don't want to be friends."

"It's too bad," Jessie said. "We thought it would be nice to have neighbors at last."

Henry nodded at his sister. "I guess we go our way, and they go their way."

So that's how it was. No new friends. No neighbors. Nothing at all.

CHAPTER 2

Benny's Plot

Benny Alden was a boy who liked to see things happen. One day at breakfast he burst out, "Those kids next door are the dumbest kids I ever saw!"

Grandfather Alden looked up in surprise. He said, "That doesn't sound like you, Benny. You are usually a kind boy."

"Well, I don't mean to hurt anybody," answered Benny. "I'm just telling you the way it is. You know what those new boys do, Grandfather?"

"No, what?"

"Nothing," said Benny. "They don't play, and they don't read. They don't work, and they don't talk to each other. The big one lies in the swing and never swings. And the little one lies on his back and just looks up at the leaves. He doesn't even go to sleep!"

"It's true, Grandfather," said Henry. He looked at Mr. Alden. "I have never seen boys like them."

Benny went on. "Here they are, two healthy boys, one eight and one ten."

"How do you know how old they are?" Jessie asked.

"I asked them. I went through our woods and looked over the hedge and asked them how old they were."

"What did they say?" asked Violet.

"Just that. Jeffrey said one word, *ten*, and Sammy said one word, *eight*. Then I said, 'Don't you ever play anything?' And they both said one word, *no*. So I came home. I was discouraged."

Henry glanced at Mr. Alden and raised his eyebrows as if asking a question. Mr. Alden nodded. Getting up from the table, he said, "I must go to work. Good luck to you all."

Then Grandfather Alden stopped and added, "I must tell you that I have an idea for a vacation later in the summer, maybe the last of July. So that gives you about three weeks to do whatever you like with the neighbors."

The four Aldens looked at their grandfather.

Benny said, "I don't suppose it's any use to ask you what your idea is?"

"No, Ben. No use at all. You know I never tell secrets."

"I know," said Henry, laughing. "Do you want me to drive you to work?"

"No, Bill will drive. But thank you just the same, Henry."

Bill was Mrs. McGregor's husband. He took care of the yard and the vegetable garden and the flowers.

When Mr. Alden had gone, the four young people still sat at the table, thinking and talking.

Benny said, "I wonder why those boys don't do anything. There is something wrong somewhere."

Violet looked at her brother and said, "Benny, I

don't think they're lazy. I think they are unhappy."

"Why?" asked Benny. "Why should they be un-happy? They have a big yard full of trees and bushes and rocks. Most boys would think it was a great place to have fun."

Violet shook her head. "I don't really know, but I think they are not very happy with their parents."

"You're right," said Jessie. "We all noticed that Mrs. Beach didn't pay any attention to the boys that time when we called on them."

At last Henry said, "Let's say they are not happy. We can't let two boys live like this right next door. We must do something about it."

Jessie agreed. "We ought to try."

"Now what could we do?" asked Violet. "Let's think."

They were quiet for a long time. Then Benny's eyes opened wide and he jumped up.

"I know! A tree house! Everybody likes a tree house, even grownups. Even the Swiss Family Robin-son! Even Robinson Crusoe!"

Jessie said, "That's right, Ben. The Beaches have plenty of trees in their backyard. Is there a good one for a tree house? We've never made a tree house ourselves!"

"It would be fun," Violet said, "even for us. You'll have to show us how, Henry. Where are the boys now?"

Jeffrey and Sammy were in their backyard, as usual. They were sitting in the swing, side by side. They were even swinging a little.

When Benny saw them, he said, "Well, that's a good sign. I never saw them swing before. Let's go and get something started."

The four Aldens went to the hedge and called, "Hello, there!"

"Hello," said the boys together. They stopped swinging.

Benny said, "You don't seem to play much or do anything."

Sammy answered, "There isn't anything special to do."

"Haven't you got bikes?" asked Henry. "I thought I saw two bikes."

"Oh, yes, we have bikes," replied Jeffrey. "But we can't go out on the highway with them. My mom says it is too dangerous."

Jessie asked, "Are you all alone? Is your mother at home?"

"No, she isn't here right now," said Jeffrey. "She's writing a book, so she has to study in the new Science Library a lot. That's why we moved here, to give Mom a nice quiet place to write in. But she doesn't know what to do with us. She said, 'You'll be perfectly safe if you stay right in the yard. And don't do anything to get into trouble.' "

"I see," Henry said. "Do you think she would mind if we came over to see you?"

Jeffrey said, "No, I don't think so. But we can't go out of this yard. Mom doesn't want us run over by a car. I know Dad would like to have you come. But he told us not to bother you because you are older than we are."

Sammy said suddenly, "Dad is a very smart man. He's a scientist. I'm going to be a scientist, too, when I grow up, just like my dad. I like to think about chlorophyll."

"About what?" Benny asked in surprise.

"Chlorophyll," repeated Sammy. "My dad says chlorophyll is the green in the leaves and that's what keeps us alive. I like to lie and look at those trees and think about that."

Benny laughed, "That's a big word for an eight-year-old," he said.

Jeffrey broke in, "I like to think about space. I'd like to run a computer and guide the men walking on the moon."

Benny said, "You boys are interested in grown-up ideas. You don't seem to want to play. Why is that?"

Jeffrey thought a minute. Then he said, "I guess it's because we haven't any friends our age."

Henry said, "Benny thought building a tree house would be fun." That was all he said, and the other Aldens waited and said nothing.

The Beach boys looked at each other and then they both began to talk at once. They were so different from the boys who never said a word.

Sammy said, "Do you know how to build one?"

"Well, I never built one," replied Henry. "But I think I could."

"That wouldn't be dangerous," shouted Sammy. "And we wouldn't get into any trouble."

"We've got lots of tools," said Jeffrey. "They are really my father's tools, but I know he will let us use them. He's very fussy about them. He put a big piece of white oilcloth on the wall in the cellar. Then he drew pictures of every tool with black ink, just exactly the size of the tools. You always have to put each tool back in the right place."

"That I'd like to see!" Benny said. "Lots of times I can't even find a hammer."

"We've got loads of boards, too!" exclaimed Sammy. "There are the big boxes in the cellar that the furniture came in. One is a piano box. We could take the boxes apart. Do you want to see them?"

The Beach boys led the Aldens down the outside
steps into the dark cellar. Jeffrey turned on the light.
There were boxes and boxes, just as Sammy said.

Henry looked at the boxes and then said, "The
floor of the tree house must be strong. Let's use the
piano box for the floor."

But Jessie said, "Wait a minute. Do you think it will be all right? Maybe Mr. or Mrs. Beach wants the piano box for something else?"

"Oh, no," replied Jeffrey. "I'm positive. I don't think they remember the boxes are in the cellar."

Sammy nodded his head. "That's right. Boxes don't mean a thing to Mom or Dad."

"Well, if you're sure, we'll begin," said Henry. "It will take a long time just to get enough boards for the floor."

The Aldens and the Beaches tugged and lifted the piano box up the cellar steps into the backyard. They set it down.

"Now for a tree," said Sammy. "I think that one would be exactly right." He pointed upward. "That would be grand for a tree house. It's a white oak."

Henry looked at Sammy. He said, "You are exactly right. It's the best tree in the whole yard."

Jessie looked at the tree and said, "I never saw a tree just like that one. Its lower branches are enormous."

"It's a special tree," said Sammy. "Dad told us that Uncle Max fell out of it once."

"Years and years ago," Jeffrey said.

"Your Uncle Max? Who is Uncle Max? Did he live here?" asked Benny.

Jeffrey looked at Sammy, and Sammy looked at Jeffrey. They laughed, and Jeffrey said, "We might as well tell you. Dad and Uncle Max are brothers, and they lived right in this house when they were boys."

"Then that's why Mr. Beach didn't seem to be a stranger in the neighborhood. We wondered about that," Henry said.

"Yes, that's why," agreed Jeffrey. "Dad is no stranger, and Uncle Max is no stranger. Grandfather bought this big house."

"It is a big house," Jessie said. "It must have twenty rooms."

Benny asked, "Was this before our grandfather bought our house?"

"Yes," Jeffrey said. "Dad told us two families lived in your house before your grandfather came here."

"Your dad and uncle must have had a good time here when they were boys," Benny said.

"They had a big fight," Jeffrey said. "Their father gave them a spyglass—a telescope, you know. It was a good one. One day they couldn't find it. My dad said my uncle took it, and Uncle Max said my dad took it. They never found the spyglass. Uncle Max and Dad never got along very well after that."

Violet said, "I don't see why a spyglass made that much difference."

"It wasn't just that," Jeffrey said. "Dad went to college, but Uncle Max wouldn't go. He was in the army for a while. When he came back he decided he'd open a restaurant. He bought a place just off the state road. He lives there all alone upstairs over the restaurant."

Benny exclaimed, "Oh, we know where that is. It's called Beach's Place."

"Right!" said Sammy. "Dad said he would take us down to see Uncle Max when he has time. But he'll never have time. I would like to go there, though, and ask Uncle Max about the spyglass."

Jeffrey shook his head. "Dad would be angry. He still thinks Uncle Max knows something about the spyglass. And maybe he does."

Sammy said, "If we have a tree house we need a spyglass."

"Well, meanwhile," said Jeffrey, "let's get to work. It's more fun to build a tree house than to wish for a spyglass."

The Aldens laughed. The Beach boys were eager to begin.

Then Jeffrey had a question. "How are we going to get up that tree to build the house?" he asked.

"Climb," said Benny. "Do you know how to climb a tree?"

Jeffrey looked at the big tree trunk. "I think it will be more fun to use a rope ladder when we get the tree house done. We can pull the ladder up after us."

"And we could have a basket," Sammy went on. "Put a rope on the basket and pull up our dinner."

Benny looked at the boys. "You surprise me. When

we came over at first you didn't say a word. And now you talk all the time."

Jeffrey thought a minute. Then he said, "I can tell you about that. My parents don't like noise. They would rather think about their work than listen to us talk. But you Aldens talk to us, so we talk to you."

"But now let's get to work," Benny said. He borrowed Jeffrey's hammer and said, "Watch. First you give a hard pound on the back of the board. Then you pound in front where the head of the nail is."

Sammy said, "But if you pound the head of the nail, it will stay in all the better."

"No, you don't pound the head of the nail. You pound just beside it. See? The board goes down and the nail comes up. Then you can pry the nail up with the claws of the hammer."

Henry went back to the Alden house to get two more hammers. Soon the backyard at the Beach house was filled with the noise of pounding.

As Jeffrey and Sammy worked, their faces grew redder and happier.

Henry said, "I think we had better get another box. There are too many of us working on one box. We'll get in each other's way."

"A good idea," said Jessie. "Somebody will pound somebody's thumb."

"Maybe his own," said Sammy.

The pile of boards grew. Henry said, "Let's put the biggest boards in one pile and the smaller ones in another. I'd smooth them off a bit if I had a plane."

"I'll get one," Jeffrey said. "It will take off the splinters."

After a while Jessie looked at her watch. "It's twelve o'clock!" she exclaimed. "We'll have to go."

Henry looked at the two piles. "I think we have enough boards for the floor. But I don't think we ought to start the tree house without asking your father and mother. After all, it's their tree."

"They won't care," Sammy said, shaking his head. "But maybe we'd better ask them just the same."

"Well, goodbye," said Jeffrey. "I'm sorry we can't work this afternoon."

"You can work alone," Benny said. "Just get more boards. We can use a lot. Do you have to get your own lunch?"

"No," Jeffrey said. "Our lunch is all ready. Mom leaves it on the table. Usually I'm not very hungry, but today I am."

So the Beach boys went inside for their lunch and the Aldens went home. Grandfather was there, and they told him what had happened. Benny let the others do most of the talking.

Suddenly Benny said, "Grandfather, do you remember a long time ago you said it was very hard to say 'I was wrong'?"

Mr. Alden laughed. "Yes, I'm sure I said that."

Benny said, "I was wrong."

"What do you mean, Benny?" asked Jessie.

"About the Beach kids," replied Benny. "I said they were dumb and they didn't do anything."

"Well, what do they do?" asked Mr. Alden.

"They *think*," said Benny. "That's what."

CHAPTER 3

With Hammer and Nails

Jessie and Violet were putting on old clothes the next morning when Henry called, "I wonder what Mr. and Mrs. Beach will say about that tree house? Maybe they'll say no. You know, they don't even want the boys to go out of the yard."

"That's different, Henry," said Benny. "I'll bet they will say yes. The kids think so anyway."

"They are lucky to have that big oak tree," said Henry. "It's just about perfect."

Benny nodded. "I didn't sleep a wink last night. I

was planning how to build the floor. If it broke, everyone would fall down."

Henry laughed. "You slept, Ben. But I know what you mean. I was thinking, too, and I drew a plan before you woke up."

Just then Mrs. McGregor called, "Breakfast!"

While the Aldens were eating, they could see Jeffrey and Sammy running around their yard. They were carrying more boards for the tree house.

"It's good to see those little guys run," Benny said. "I didn't know they could run. Remember?"

"We didn't know they could even move," said Jessie, laughing. "But they can do anything if they have a good reason."

"Let's not keep them waiting," Henry said, pushing back his chair.

Benny said, "If they are carrying boards, probably their parents said yes."

The Aldens went through the bushes to find the two boys waiting for them. They stood quietly, looking at the Aldens.

"What did your mom say about the tree house?"

Jeffrey answered, "She said, 'I don't care what you do, as long as you don't go out of the yard.' "

"Well, then," said Benny, "you can build the house, can't you?"

"Yes, we can," said Sammy, looking happier all of a sudden. "My dad is different. He made a little plan. He seemed to be interested. Jeffrey and I made plans, too. But I think Dad's is the best." He gave it to Henry.

"Now, let's see," Henry said, holding the plans so everyone could see. He looked at Jessie and laughed. "I guess Ben wasted his sleepless night. Mr. Beach's plan is just perfect."

The Aldens bent over to look at Mr. Beach's drawing. The trunk of the tree made the back of the house.

"Now let's look at the boys' plan," Henry said.

Everyone began to laugh. Jeffrey and Sammy had put in so many things they had forgotten the tree. There was a pail hanging on a pulley and a lunch

basket hanging on a rope. There was a fine dinner bell
by the door—only there wasn't any door. The boys
had drawn a peek hole in the roof, a lantern, and a
mailbox. They had two hammocks for beds and a
spyglass.

Henry said, "I guess you are right, Sammy. Your
dad's plan is the best of all. You put all the last things
first—and the first things not at all."

"Don't feel sorry, boys," Violet said quickly.
"You aren't so very old, you know, and your father is
a scientist. He ought to draw a better plan than you
can."

Jeffrey said suddenly, "It's really the tree that's the
best. When you look at all the other trees, you can
see how good it is."

"Right!" said Benny. "Jeffrey, you are exactly
right. This tree couldn't be better. Those big
branches are almost level. We can just put the heavy
floor beams across and they will stay without any
nails."

"We'll nail them just the same," Henry said. "By

the way, how did your father know about the branches?"

"He came out with a flashlight after we had gone to bed," said Sammy. "We saw the light. He just took one look and came right back in the house. He told us this morning, 'That tree is just made for a tree house. I wish I could stay and help you build it.' That's what he said."

"I wish he could, too," Jeffrey said. "But of course he never has any time to play. He has to work even when he's at home. Now let's really begin, Henry."

"Well, all right. Now Ben, you climb the tree. Then I'll pass the heavy beams up to you. They are too heavy for Sam and Jeff."

"It is awfully high," Sammy said. "But of course not too high."

Henry smiled because for Sammy it was a little too high.

Four long beams were soon resting on the lowest of the big branches. Henry himself nailed them safely in place. Then he showed Jeffrey and Sam how to lay the floorboards. The boards from the piano box were smooth and all the same length. They made a good floor.

"Now you boys have fun for yourselves. Put in a nice flat floor," Henry said. Then he climbed down.

Sammy said, "Let's put the nails in my basket and pull it up." So after all, the basket on the rope was the first thing in the tree house instead of the last.

Jeffrey laid the boards and Sammy stayed by his side and gave him the nails one by one. Benny climbed down and handed up more floorboards. He called up to Sammy, "You can live there just as soon as you have a roof over your heads."

"I think we can live here just as soon as we have a floor under our feet," said Sammy.

Benny began to swing himself up the tree, holding onto the smaller of the lowest branches. Sammy looked up and watched him. He said, "I think we need a ladder. We'll have to go up and down lots of times, and the girls can't climb anyway."

"Oh, yes, they can!" answered Benny.

Violet looked up and said, "I think we do need a ladder just the same. We can climb, but we can work faster with a ladder. And we want to get the house done."

The Aldens turned to see Jeffrey running to the cellar for a ladder. That settled it.

Soon Henry went up the ladder and looked around. "This is certainly a big tree, Ben," he said. "It can easily hold a house for four people."

"Then we'll come up, too," Jeffrey called from the ground. He went up the ladder. His brother followed him.

"It's nice up here," said Jeffrey. "With all these big branches people can't see us from the ground."

Mr. McGregor had been mowing the Alden's lawn and watching. He could see what a good time everyone was having. He called out, "You are doing a fine job, boys!"

Sammy called back, "Thanks, Mr. McGregor. You know, this is going to be a dandy floor. It's going to have a wall-to-wall carpet."

"Really?" Mr. McGregor stopped mowing.

"Yes, sir! We have an old rug in the cellar. We can cut it to fit."

"A grand idea," agreed Mr. McGregor. "Not many tree houses have carpets."

But Jeffrey went on working on the floor, so Sammy stopped talking and handed him more nails.

Violet went up the ladder to look. "You are doing well," she said. "You are real carpenters."

In another hour the floor was done. "Now," said Sammy, "I wish we had a spyglass."

"So do I," said Jeffrey. "I wonder if Uncle Max could tell us anything about the one that was lost."

Henry and Jessie looked at each other. Jessie said, "Couldn't you go on your bikes to see Uncle Max if we all went with you?"

"Maybe!" said Sammy, eagerly. "Wouldn't that be fun—we haven't used our bikes at all."

"Ask your dad if you can go tomorrow," said Benny. "Tell him we will take good care of you."

Henry said, "Be sure to say we will be on the Shore

Road, not on the highway. There isn't much traffic."

Jeffrey looked up. He said, "Dad knows that already. About the traffic, I mean. Mom and Dad think that is the trouble with Uncle Max's restaurant. All the traffic goes on the state highway."

"I see," said Benny. "Not many people eat at the diner."

Henry said, "I think we have done enough for today."

"Then we have to pick up our tools," said Sammy.

Benny laughed. "You're the youngest, but you are the one to think of picking up the tools."

Sammy replied, "If we don't, we can't use the tools. My dad says fine tools always get fine care."

They all worked picking up the tools and boards. Then Henry started for home. He said, "Boys, remember to ask your father if you can go tomorrow. We can start rather early, and maybe put up the sides of the house when we get home."

"Don't worry," said Sammy. "My dad won't get in the door before I ask him."

Jeffrey looked at Sammy and shook his head. "You know Dad doesn't like to have us pester him. He'll say no if you tease. Just ask him quietly, and then maybe he will let us go."

"I won't bother him," Sammy promised. "I'll just say please, and tell him the Aldens are going, too."

"We don't need to tell Dad anything about the spyglass," Jeffrey said. "It might make him angry at Uncle Max all over again. I wonder if Uncle Max will know us. He hasn't seen us for a long time."

"He's older than Dad," said Sammy. "I think he will remember us if we tell him. And he'll remember the spyglass, if Dad does."

That same evening Benny said, "I wonder why those kids are so eager to have a spyglass."

"I wonder, too," said Violet. "But we all like different things. They seem to think a spyglass goes with a tree house. And it does, of course."

Benny said, "I think it's the mystery of the spyglass that gets them. They want the spyglass because it's lost and they can't find it. I'd like to find it myself."

CHAPTER 4

Finding Uncle Max

Jeffrey and Sammy Beach were running around their yard early the next morning when the Aldens were eating breakfast.

"Good luck to all of you," Mr. Alden said as he started for his car. "I hope the boys can go with you on your bicycle trip."

"Well, they act happy," said Benny. "I bet they can go."

When the boys saw the Aldens coming, they were too excited to take turns speaking. "Yes, we can go on our bikes!" Jeffrey shouted. "Mom said so. We were so surprised! And we don't even have to get back for lunch. We can buy lunch at Uncle Max's restaurant."

"We each have a dollar," said Sammy.

"Good," said Jessie. "We'll go back for our bikes."

The Aldens went home to get their bikes and to tell Mrs. McGregor that they would not be home for lunch.

"We'll eat lunch at that little diner just off the Shore Road," said Jessie.

Mrs. McGregor nodded. She said, "I'm glad the two boys are going to have a bit of exercise—and get out of that backyard for once."

"Yes," Jessie agreed. "Mr. and Mrs. Beach don't think much about what young boys like to do. I have a feeling they just expect Jeffrey and Sam to be as little trouble as possible."

"They don't want to be bothered," agreed Mrs. McGregor. "That's easy to see."

Soon six bicycles were wheeled out to the street. Benny stayed close to Sammy and began to talk to him. "Sammy," he said, "tell me why you want that spyglass so much."

"Every tree house ought to have a spyglass,"

Sammy answered him. "You have to watch out for the enemy. And you want to see anything moving in the woods."

"Yes, but most people build their house first and then get a telescope," said Benny. "Now you boys wanted one before we even started the tree house. Why?"

"Well, you see we knew Uncle Max and Dad had one once," Sammy told him, "and we might as well find it."

Benny thought this over. He knew it was no reason at all. But now the others were pedaling down the street on their way to the Shore Road. Benny and Sammy followed.

It was very pleasant riding along the country road. There were no hills, and the road was smooth. It was not too hot, and there was a salt breeze blowing off the ocean. The six riders kept together very well. Sometimes one was ahead and sometimes another.

After they had been riding for about an hour, Benny was ahead. Suddenly he turned in a half-circle and came back to the rest. He said, "I will not go another pedal without something to eat."

Violet laughed and said, "I'm glad you said that, Benny. I'm hungry, too."

Jeffrey said, "Well, anyway I'm tired. Aren't we near Uncle Max's place yet?"

"Yes, we are," replied Henry. "I have driven past it in the car, but never stopped to eat there. It's right around this bend."

Benny said, "Well, I can wait that long." And they rode along to the bend in the road.

"Here it is, Jeffrey," said Henry. "BEACH'S PLACE." He pointed to an old sign. It was broken and hard to read.

The four boys and two girls parked their bikes by the steps.

"Sammy and I never saw this place before," said Jeffrey. "Uncle Max must be an old guy. He's much older than my dad. I hope he will know who we are."

"Don't worry," said Benny. "Just tell him. He'll believe you. And if he doesn't, *we'll* tell him."

They went in. The room was rather dark and it was empty, but there was a fine smell of hamburger cooking.

Then a man came out of the back room of the restaurant. He was not an old guy at all. He was lively and strong, never still a minute. He had curly gray hair and bright blue eyes. He smiled at his customers and said, "Do you want sandwiches or hot dogs or hamburgers?"

Nobody answered, but Sammy stepped up to the counter and looked up at the man.

"Are you Uncle Max?" he asked. "I'm Sammy."

"Bless my soul!" said Max Beach. "Are you really? The last time I saw you, I held you in my arms. You were a tiny baby. Where is your brother?"

"Right here," Jeffrey said. "Then we both have been in this very room?"

"Yes, you have, Jeffrey. But you were too small to remember it. And how is your father? And your mother?"

"They're very busy," answered Sammy. "But Dad says he is coming to see you soon."

"I hope so," Mr. Beach replied. "I know he is an important scientist now. He won't have much time for me, I'm afraid."

"Well, don't worry," said Sammy. "He doesn't have much time for us either. These are our new neighbors, the Aldens. They take lots of time with us."

The Aldens smiled at Mr. Beach.

Benny said, "These boys are worth a lot of time. We are all building a tree house."

"A tree house!" Uncle Max exclaimed. "Now that's interesting! Are you building it in the big oak tree?"

"That's right!" said Benny. "How did you guess?"

"Well, I'll tell you all about it, but you must have something to eat first. You look hungry to me."

Violet laughed, "Yes, we are. I want a hamburger, a big one!"

"We'd all like hamburgers," said Jessie. "And milk for everybody."

"I'll be back in a jiffy," said Uncle Max. "Everything is ready. Excuse me for a minute."

The visitors looked around. The room was quite dark. There was one big table and two smaller ones with chairs. Then there was the counter with stools. They all sat on the stools.

Soon Mr. Beach came in with a tray. He put six
plates with hamburgers on the counter and poured six
glasses of milk. He sat down on the other side of the
counter.

Jeffrey said, chewing, "This isn't just a hamburger,
Uncle Max. This is a whole dinner. French fried
potatoes, lettuce, tomatoes, and salad dressing and
pickles!"

"Yes, I know," Uncle Max nodded. "I like to see
people eat. And now tell me about the tree house."

"We began it two days ago, Mr. Beach," said
Henry. "The boys just finished the floor."

"You call me Uncle Max, too, will you? Now I bet
you children came down to see about that old spyglass."

Everybody laughed because Uncle Max was laughing. "Such a silly thing!" he said. "I suppose your
father forgot about it long ago."

"Oh, no, he didn't!" said Sammy. "He still says
you have it."

"Well, I haven't," said Uncle Max. "I have no idea

where it is. And now I guess you want it for your tree house."

"Well, we'd certainly like it," said Sammy, drinking his milk. "A tree house always has a spyglass."

"Well, that is true," agreed Mr. Beach. "Let me tell you something you don't seem to know. Your father and I had a tree house in that very tree."

"You did?" exclaimed Benny. "Nobody told us that."

"No, my dad never told us," said Jeffrey. "I don't know why. I guess he was too busy. He's always working."

"We didn't have it very long because we moved away," Uncle Max went on. "But it was a pretty fine tree house. And that's where we used the spyglass. We were very careful of it because it was a good one. It was in a heavy leather case. We always put it back in the case."

"Did you and Mr. Beach do all the work on the tree house yourselves?" asked Benny.

"Well, almost. We had trouble with the roof. We

weren't tall enough, so a man helped us a couple of times. He was visiting the people who lived in your house then."

"Maybe that man took the telescope," said Jeffrey.

"Oh, no! He wouldn't steal a penny, I'm sure of that. He wasn't there very long, anyway. He came and went in a month, and we never saw him again."

Henry looked at Uncle Max and asked, "Did you miss the spyglass just after he helped you?"

Uncle Max did not want to answer this. But he said, "Well, I must say yes. We missed it the very day he went away. But he didn't steal it. I'm absolutely sure! He had a telescope of his own, anyway."

Violet said, "I don't think Henry meant that the man stole it. But he may have put it somewhere."

"Maybe," said Uncle Max. "We never found it, anyway. The man made a hole in the roof so we could lie down in the tree house at night and look at the stars."

"What a dandy idea!" exclaimed Sammy. "We're going to do that, too, aren't we, Benny?"

"Yes, sir," said Benny. "We'll have a hole in the roof even if we don't have a spyglass!"

Jeffrey was thinking. He looked at his uncle and said, "The spyglass was one reason you didn't get along with my dad?"

"Yes, part of the reason. I didn't like school very much, but your dad always did well. There was a war then, and I wanted to be in the army. Your dad went to college. We didn't see each other for many years. When the war was over, I traveled around for a while. Then I came back here and bought this diner. Your father and mother came to see me once. Sammy was a baby, and Jeffrey was too little to remember."

"That must have been when we were living in New York," Jeffrey said. "But New York is so noisy and busy that Mom doesn't like it any more. She didn't like to walk to the library, and she didn't like to drive."

"And Dad found the old house in Greenfield was empty—so we moved," said Sammy.

"I'm glad you did," said Uncle Max. Then he

looked from Jeffrey to Sammy. "I used to think it was kind of a spooky old house. It sounds funny, but I always felt better in our tree house than anywhere else. You boys feel that way?"

"No," Jeffrey said. "Of course we haven't any tree house yet. We haven't had much chance to explore the house. Mostly we stay outside."

"I used to hear a queer rocking sound," Uncle Max said, more to himself than to the boys. "People used to tell stories about families who had lived in the house a long time ago. They were always sad stories. But things must be different today. And now, how about some apple pie for dessert?"

"Yes," said Henry. "We always take apple pie when we can. We want to see if it is as good as Jessie's. She made one once with a glass bottle for a rolling pin."

Uncle Max laughed and went out to get dessert. He soon came back. They were all eating the delicious pie when Sammy said, "All this fuss about a spyglass!"

"Well, it wasn't just the spyglass," said Uncle Max. "Your father was smart and he's really a great man. I am not smart like that, and I've never made much money. This diner isn't doing very well. You can see there aren't any other customers."

"Yes, we noticed that," said Jessie. "I'm sorry."

"Thank you," said Uncle Max. "I wish my brother and I could be friends, but if he is too busy, that's that."

"We'll tell him what a good lunch we had," said Jeffrey. Both Beach boys took out their money.

"No sir!" cried Uncle Max. "You're invited to lunch. I won't take a cent from any of you. It was a pleasure to talk to you."

Even Henry could not make Uncle Max change his mind, so they thanked him again and rode away.

"We'll be back soon," they all called.

"Now isn't that the funniest thing!" said Benny. "Nobody has the spyglass. It must really be lost."

"We can use our old field glasses to look at the birds," said Jessie. "But a telescope would be better."

"We'll make do," said Benny. "And we still have a little time to work on the tree house this afternoon."

Benny was right. Before Mr. and Mrs. Beach came home, they finished one whole side of the tree house, leaving a square hole for a window.

"We're doing fine!" exclaimed Sammy. "The back is done, because that's the tree, and the front will be open. That leaves only one side to do!"

Henry said, "When we get the roof on, you can live up there."

Sammy added, "By that time we'll have my carpet in."

Just then they were all surprised. The back door of the house opened, and Mrs. Beach came out.

"Mom! You're home!" cried the boys.

"Stay right there," said Mrs. Beach. "Here is your supper. We'll send it up in the basket. Wait till we say 'Ready'."

The Beach boys climbed into the tree house and let down the basket. The Aldens went to meet Mrs. Beach, and Henry took the heavy tray.

Mrs. Beach said, "Benny, you eat with them the first time. They will enjoy it more."

Benny said, "So will I. It looks delicious, Mrs. Beach."

First the boys pulled up fried chicken, raw carrots, and paper plates in the basket. Then they let it down, and Benny put in rolls, cookies, and a bowl of chocolate pudding. The third time they pulled up a carton of milk and three plastic cups. Then Benny went up to join the supper party.

Jessie said, "We'll leave them alone, Mrs. Beach. They will have a better time with no girls."

"You have been good to my boys," said Mrs. Beach. "Sometime we will have a talk. My husband and I are very grateful to you."

Jessie was just going to tell Mrs. Beach about their trip to see Uncle Max. But she stopped in time. The boys surely ought to tell their parents about Uncle Max and the lost telescope.

CHAPTER 5

Up a Tree

Then for two days it rained. Benny and Henry put on their raincoats and went over to see Sammy and Jeffrey.

Henry showed them how to make a sign for the tree house with their names on it, so they had something to do. Benny showed them how to tie knots in a rope. They could use it to climb up to the tree house and pull it in after them.

While the boys were working with the rope they began to talk to Benny. Jeffrey said, "Remember how Uncle Max said the old house seemed spooky?"

"Yes," Benny answered. "But it doesn't seem spooky to you, does it?"

Sammy said, "Maybe sometimes it does. Last night when I was in bed I heard it storming and blowing outside. Then right over my head I heard a funny sort of rocking sound—just what Uncle Max said. I felt scared and got Jeffrey. I didn't want to bother Mom or Dad. They don't like to be waked up for nothing."

"That's right," Jeffrey said. "But I didn't hear anything. I told him it was just his imagination. I bet Uncle Max imagined it, too."

"But you went up to the attic with me to look around this morning," Sammy said. "You wanted to see if there was anything that would rock."

"Was there?" asked Benny.

Jeffrey shook his head. "We couldn't find anything. It was just Sammy's imagination."

"Maybe," Sammy said.

At last the sun came out again, bright and warm. The boys went out at once and soon finished the other wall of the house.

The next day they began to make the roof. First

they stood in a row on the ground and looked up.

"Doesn't it look wonderful?" said Jeffrey. "I'm glad the roof doesn't have a point at the top."

"Your dad was clever," Henry agreed. "A slanting roof is much quicker and easier to build. And it makes a roof out over the porch, too."

Sammy said, "We can even sit on the porch when it rains—if the rain comes straight down."

Benny added, "The rain will run back toward the tree—and not down your necks."

Henry picked up the longest board he had. He climbed up and started to put in the long runners. "When these runners are in, you boys can start fitting in the roof."

"Don't you think it will leak?" asked Jeffrey.

"Well, it may," Henry called down. "But that's the fun of a tree house. You can always make it better."

"I'll get the carpet," said Sammy. "Maybe we can put it in today, if we get the roof on."

Jessie and Violet helped him measure the floor.

Then they helped him cut the rug to fit. It was ready to tack down as soon as the roof was done.

Soon the two Beach boys were pounding away on their roof.

"Don't hurry," advised Benny.

"I'm not hurrying," answered Sammy. "We have all day to get the roof on. Then the house will be done."

But a little later Sammy stopped working.

Benny thought, "He's tired. After all, he is only eight years old."

But Sammy was not tired. He was sitting on a branch looking up at something. At last he said, "Benny, there's a big knothole up in this branch. I think I can reach it. Maybe there are baby squirrels in it or baby woodpeckers."

"Wait," Benny called. "I'm coming up, too. But watch out! Squirrels have sharp teeth."

Before Benny could get up the tree, Sammy was already standing on tiptoes, reaching into the hole as far as he could with his hand.

There was something. It wasn't a squirrel. It wasn't a woodpecker. What was it? Sammy pulled his hand out. "I know I felt something, Ben!" he said.

"Well, try again, Sammy. Pull it out if you can."

Sammy took a deep breath and put his hand back in the hole. "Here goes, everybody!"

His fingers did touch something. It wasn't soft. It was hard and smooth. Sammy stretched a little higher. Dry leaves and dust fell from the hole.

"Here's something else!" Sammy said. He pulled out what looked like a long crooked twig. It was twisted and hard. "It's a piece of leather, I think," Sammy said.

He handed it to Ben. "Sure is," Benny agreed. "Only it's rotted. What else can you find? Maybe this is part of a strap."

Sammy dug down into the hole again, took a tight hold, and pulled.

Out came something long, and shaped like a box. "This is pretty heavy," said Sammy. "What is it? It's dirty, that's sure."

"Well, this looks like a case for one thing," Benny said. "See? It's made of the same leather as the other piece. What do you suppose is in it?" Benny found two buckles on it and began to open the case.

"It's been there a long time," Henry said.

"I have a guess," Benny said. The case fell open.

"Oh!" everyone said. "The spyglass!"

"Sammy, you take this end and pull," Benny said. "And Jeffrey, you hold the other end."

Sammy held onto his end and started to pull.

"Pull it way out, Sam," Henry called from below.

"You know what?" said Jeffrey. "This must be the lost spyglass. It has to be!"

"But how did it get *here?*" Jeffrey asked.

"Remember the man who helped your dad and Uncle Max build their tree house?" Henry asked. "He must have put it there himself while he was working on the roof. He probably forgot to tell the boys."

"I think that was the way it was," nodded Benny. "Let me have a look."

He drew out the telescope a little farther and looked all around. He could even see the next field through the oak leaves.

Benny pointed the spyglass toward the Beach house. He looked at the roof. He could see every shingle. Then he saw a round window near the roof.

"I've never seen that round window before," Benny said, puzzled.

"Let me look," Jeffrey said. "Our house hasn't any round windows, just square ones."

"Well, there it is," Benny said. "You can see it, too."

Jeffrey and Sam took turns looking through the telescope. The window was at the back of the house, on the third floor.

"Just where is it, Ben?" Jessie called.

"It must be in the attic," Benny said.

Henry, Violet, and Jessie looked up. They tried to see through the branches. Henry called, "We can't see any round window from here. The trees are in the way and so is the porch roof."

"Well, you can see it from here," said Jeffrey. "It is made of colored glass."

Henry climbed up the tree and took the glass. And there was the little round window up near the roof. It was made of blue and green and red glass.

Then Henry climbed down and Jessie climbed up. She saw the window at once.

Benny said, "One thing is sure. You can see that window from the tree, but you can't see it from the ground."

Jeffrey nodded. He said, "You can't see it from inside the house, either. Sammy and I explored that rainy day. We went all over the attic. We use that top floor to put things in. Mom hung some clothes there on hooks."

"Come on," said Sammy. "Let's all go into the house and hunt for that window."

Jessie shook her head. "No, Sammy, I don't think we Aldens had better go. You'd better wait and ask your parents first. You two boys could go alone, though."

"No!" said both boys at once. Sammy shook his head firmly. "It wouldn't be any fun without you Aldens. But if we ask, will you go with us?"

"Of course," said Benny. "I don't think we ought to hunt around in anyone's house without their knowing."

"I suppose not," said Jeffrey. "I suppose we ought to finish the roof."

They finished the roof, but they could hardly wait for their family to come home.

Jeffrey said, "We seem to spend all our time asking Mom if we can do this and that! I do wish we could go up in that attic right now."

Benny said smiling, "You're not the only one, Jeffrey! I'm dying to go!"

CHAPTER 6

Behind the Round Window

M r. and Mrs. Beach were hardly in the house when Jeffrey and Sam told them about the round window.

"That is a mystery," said Mr. Beach. "I can't remember any round window. And Max and I never saw it from the tree house we built."

The boys took their father out and showed him how they could see the window from the tree house. Mr. Beach looked at the tree and then he said, "I know why Max and I never saw that window. There was a big branch in the way. See? There is a scar where the branch was cut off."

"May we ask Benny and the others and go up in the attic now?" Sammy asked. "The Aldens didn't want to come in without asking you."

"Yes, it will be all right," Mr. Beach answered. "I haven't time to help you."

Jeffrey telephoned the Aldens, and Benny said he would come right over. Jessie and Henry were away, but he and Violet could come.

It was late afternoon when the two Aldens and the Beaches climbed the attic stairs.

Violet said, "I just can't understand where that window can be when no one knows anything about it."

Jeffrey explained, "The attic is so big it has been made into rooms. It is really more like a third floor than an attic. The walls are plastered and papered. You'll see."

Benny looked all around at the top of the stairs. That side of the attic had been made into two rooms.

The first room was large, but it was empty.

"I think someone lived up on this floor," Benny said. "You can see the nail holes at the windows where there were rods for curtains."

Violet said, "There's some wallpaper, too."

Jeffrey said, "But there aren't any electric lights up here."

Sammy said, "We think the house was built before there were electric lights. People must have used lamps or maybe candles."

Violet looked at the dark corners of the empty room. It was certainly a spooky place. Violet noticed that everyone was beginning to whisper. The air was dry and stuffy.

The four children went into the next room. They found only some old boxes and chairs. They were dusty and faded.

"Never mind this side of the house," said Jeffrey. "The round window is at the back of the house."

Sammy said, "There's a very large clothes closet. It's almost as big as a room."

"That's what we want to see," said Benny.

There was a door to the closet. It had a glass doorknob. Jeffrey opened it and they all went in.

"Oh, look at the wallpaper!" Violet exclaimed. "I never saw anything like it."

It was beautiful old paper with pictures of toys on it: balls and horns and drums. The colors were still bright. There was one big window, but it was not round. Mrs. Beach had hung some dresses on a row of hooks on the wall, and there were piles of old books and boxes on the floor.

Sammy said, "Those are hatboxes. Mom's winter hats are in them. I carried them up for her, but I didn't look at the wallpaper. I thought this was just an old attic to put things in."

"Let's open the window," Benny suggested.

It wasn't easy to open the window, but the boys did it. Benny leaned out as far as he safely could.

"I see it! I see the round window!" he called into the attic room to the others. Then he added, "That's funny."

Benny pulled his head in and looked around him. "The round window is just beyond this closet window."

"How can it be?" Jeffrey asked. "This wall of the closet is the end of the house."

Jeffrey and Sammy and Violet took turns looking out of the open window. They each saw the round window.

Violet said, "Maybe the round window isn't a real window. Maybe it is just trimming on the outside of the house."

Benny shook his head. "It looks like a real window to me. Come on, let's look around while it's still light up here."

Benny began to tap on the wall. It was the wall that Jeffrey and Sam had thought was the end of the attic.

"What are you doing?" asked Sammy.

"Does this sound like a plaster wall?" Benny said. "Listen!"

Violet looked surprised. "It sounds like wood or something hollow," she said. "Oh, Benny, do you think someone boarded up part of the attic? But why?"

"Let's find out," Jeffrey said.

"Make a hole," Sammy suggested.

Benny held up his hand. "Wait," he said. "Let's tap all along here. You can run your hand over the wall and maybe you can feel something."

It was Sammy who said, "Something is different here, Benny. There's a long crack. What does that mean?"

"Another crack over here," Jeffrey called.

Benny said, "That means just one thing. A door. The door must be papered right over."

Violet said, "Somebody must have taken the knob off. I wonder what's on the other side. Oh, it's a little scary, isn't it?"

"Let's open it!" Sammy and Jeffrey both cried.

"Wait," Benny said. "Run and ask first."

The two Beach boys raced to find their mother, who was getting dinner.

"A door papered over?" she said. "I can hardly

believe that! Yes, you can try to open it. I'm sure you'll just find an empty space and plenty of dust."

"Get something to cut the paper with," Sammy said.

"A screwdriver," Jeffrey said.

Benny and Violet were waiting for the boys. Although the sun had not set, the attic was getting dark. Violet could imagine she heard a rocking noise on the other side of the hidden door. She wished that Mr. or Mrs. Beach would come upstairs, too.

"Here, Benny," Jeffrey called. "I have a screwdriver. Mom doesn't think we'll find anything, though."

"We'll soon see," Benny said. He ran the screwdriver along the two cracks. Then he climbed on a stool and ran the screwdriver along the top of the hidden door. The paper was already loose at the bottom, near the floor.

"Now, everybody push!" Benny said. "The hinges must be on the other side. The door should swing into the hidden room, if there is one."

But although Violet, Benny, Jeffrey, and Sammy pushed as hard as they could, nothing happened.

"It must be nailed shut," Benny said, disappointed.

Jeffrey gave the door another push. "It rattles a little," he said. "And hear that soft rocking?" He put his ear to the crack.

"I'm dumb!" Benny said. "Here, give me the screwdriver again. Where could that door catch be?"

Violet felt along the edges of the door. "Here," she said. "I can feel a little hole where the doorknob was."

Benny pried carefully and pushed back the door catch. "Now let's try again!" he said.

There was a push and the door suddenly opened. All four of the children nearly fell into the gloomy space on the other side.

Violet drew in her breath. Something seemed to move gently in the shadows. On tiptoe they all stepped into the room. It was bigger than they had expected, but the only light came in from the round window.

"It's a boy's room," exclaimed Jeffrey.

Then Violet said, "Look! Over in that spot of light! A rocking horse! How big it is."

"As big as a real pony," said Sammy. "It looks like a wooden horse on a merry-go-round."

He touched the horse's wooden nose and it rocked gently. "This is what I heard. My room is right under the attic here. It wasn't my imagination!"

And before anyone could stop him, Sammy was on the horse's back, riding back and forth, a fine high ride, bump, bump, bump.

"This is exactly the bump," said Sammy, nodding. "Only it's louder when I'm riding the horse. The wind must blow in a little and make it rock gently."

Benny, Jeffrey, and Violet were looking all around the room. There was a boy's bed with sides. A red blanket was folded at the foot of the bed. A large stuffed dog printed on cloth lay against the pillow. A toy monkey sat in a small chair. There were books and pictures and a pair of boy's red leather slippers.

Jeffrey picked up the slippers. "These are too small

for Sammy," he said. "The boy must have been younger than eight."

"And who was he?" asked Violet. "He must have had this room a long, long time ago."

Benny said, "A mystery room for sure."

"I'm going to call Dad," said Jeffrey. "He'll want to see this room, and maybe he'll have an idea."

Jeffrey went to the stairs and called, "Dad! Can you come up to the attic?"

Soon both Mr. and Mrs. Beach came up the stairs and looked into the mystery room. It was getting darker, but they could see enough to be surprised.

"Well, well," said Mr. Beach. "You did find something by using that telescope, didn't you? I never knew a thing about this room."

"How can we find out who the little boy was?" asked Benny.

Mr. Beach was thinking. "I know one thing we can try. Uncle Max is older than I am. He might have a clue. Tomorrow is Saturday. We can drive down to see Max. I want to tell him you found the spyglass."

Sam and Jeff were too surprised to say a word. Their parents were really going to take them to see Uncle Max.

"This is a beautiful room for a little boy," said Mrs. Beach. "I wonder who he was and what happened to him. And why did somebody try to hide his room?"

Benny said, "Maybe something happened to him. He might have been sick or even died."

"And then it was too sad to see his old room," Violet went on. She felt unhappy thinking about it.

But it turned out that Benny and Violet were not right at all.

CHAPTER 7

More Questions

Benny and Violet told Henry, Jessie, and Mr. Alden all about the secret room in the attic. Everyone tried to guess why the room had been closed, but no one had any new ideas.

Benny said, "Mr. Beach thought Uncle Max might have a clue. He's going to take Mrs. Beach and the boys to see Uncle Max tomorrow. He wants to explain about the telescope. He asked if we would come, too."

"I'd like to," Jessie said. "But do you think we'd be in the way? I'm sure Sammy and Jeffrey haven't had their mother and father take them anywhere very often."

Henry said, "The boys think their parents are more interested in their work than in the things their sons do. It's too bad."

"But Mr. Beach asked us," Benny said. "Their car won't hold all of us. Henry, why don't you drive our station wagon?"

That was the way it turned out. Violet and Benny looked at each other when Mr. Beach said, "Come, Sammy. You sit with me. Then we can talk. Jeffrey, you hold the spyglass and sit with your mother."

As Henry started the car he heard Mr. Beach say, "I wish Max were doing better with his restaurant. So few people use the Shore Road that he hasn't any customers."

Jeffrey nodded. "That's right. But he's the best cook in the world."

Sammy said, "And Uncle Max likes to see people

enjoy his cooking. It makes him happy."

"The trouble is that Max won't let anyone help him," Mr. Beach said.

Suddenly Sammy said, "Maybe we can help him with some ideas. I think that would be all right."

"Perhaps you're right," said Mrs. Beach.

Uncle Max could hardly believe his eyes when the car drove up to his door. He came down the steps and shook hands with his brother.

He said, "John, how wonderful to see you! Welcome, everybody, and come right in."

Sammy said, "We told you we'd be back."

"Yes, you did. And I knew you would, too. Come and sit down."

Sammy couldn't wait any longer. "Look, Uncle Max—here's the telescope!"

"You found it? Where?" asked Uncle Max looking in surprise from Sammy to Jeffrey.

"In a knothole in the oak tree," Jeffrey said.

"Well!" Uncle Max said, and then he thought a moment. "I believe the man from next door who helped us build our tree house must have put the telescope in the knothole. He just forgot to tell us. I'm sure now it was that kind man."

Mr. Beach said, "That's what we think, too, Max. I didn't have it, and you didn't have it. Nobody had it." And he shook hands with his brother again.

"And we've got more news. A surprise and a mystery!" Sammy sat down on a stool and whirled around. Everyone else sat down at the big table.

"Sammy is right," said his father. "It is a mystery. Let the boys tell it. Maybe you can help solve it."

The two boys told about the round window and how they could see it with the telescope. Then they told about the hidden room and all the toys.

Uncle Max began to frown. "Oh, I wish I could remember," he exclaimed. "I never knew about that room. But I did know the name of the family who lived there long ago. Now what was it?"

"Try the alphabet," said Jeffrey.

They all laughed, but Uncle Max began. "The name didn't begin with A. And it didn't begin with B. Now, C! I think it must have been C. Cook? Collins? No, those names aren't right."

"Cooper," suggested Mrs. Beach.

"Carter," said Jessie.

"Wait!" Uncle Max said. "Carter sounds almost right. Let me think. I know. Carver! That's the name. I'm sure of it."

Everybody looked happy and clapped.

"My father told me that a family named Carver built the house many years ago. It was at least a hundred years old when we lived in it."

"Too bad I wasn't interested in such things when I was a boy," Mr. Beach said. "Can you remember anything else that might give the children a clue about the room?"

Max shook his head. "I'll try to think of something else. But if I were there, I'd hunt some more in that room. There might be letters or papers or something else that would be a clue."

His brother laughed and said, "I'm sure the boys and the Aldens will go over every inch of that room, Max. And now let's talk about you."

Uncle Max looked unhappy. "The diner isn't doing very well," he said. "But that's not your worry, it's mine."

"It's mine," said Sammy. "I want to worry about you, Uncle Max."

"Thank you, Sammy," said Uncle Max. "I suppose I ought to close the diner and work at something else. But I do love to cook and see people eat."

Mrs. Beach said, "Then you should not close the restaurant, Max. People ought to do the things they like to do. Never mind just working for money."

Benny looked around. He said, "I think people like to eat where it's bright. It seems dark here."

Jeffrey added, "Maybe a new name would help. We used to go to the Jumping Jack Restaurant in New York just because we liked the name. The food wasn't as good as yours."

Jessie said, "I think people have forgotten about your place because they don't use this road much any more. You need to do something special to make them want to come."

"I could try a new name," said Uncle Max. "And I could put in more windows myself."

The Beaches and the Aldens talked about the restaurant until lunchtime. Then John Beach found out what delicious food his brother could cook. He and his wife had a chicken salad, but all the children had hot dogs.

When Henry and Mr. Beach started to pay Uncle Max, he said, "Oh, no! You are invited to lunch."

Henry said, "No. It is silly for you to take in eight people for nothing."

"My grandfather wouldn't like it if we didn't pay," Benny said.

Uncle Max had to take the money.

When they were riding home, Jeffrey said, "Let's go right up to the room and hunt around again. We might find something we missed."

"And I haven't even seen it," Henry said.

"Nor I!" Jessie added.

CHAPTER 8

Mrs. McGregor's Clue

Jessie and Henry looked around the little room that Violet, Benny, and the Beach boys had found. It looked brighter and not as spooky in the afternoon light. The big rocking horse still had some of its gay colors.

"How shall we begin?" Sammy asked.

Henry said, "Suppose you two boys take the bed. Look at everything. Don't miss a thing. Take off all the bedclothes and the mattress."

Sammy said, "I know. Maybe there's something hidden in the mattress. Come on, Jeffrey."

"Be careful," Jessie warned. "These things are old and some of them may break."

Henry said, "Violet and Jessie can take the desk. Benny and I can look at the rest of the room."

Jeffrey and Sammy pulled the bed away from the wall. They took the blanket off. They shook the pillow. They pulled the sheet back and looked at the mattress.

After a few minutes Jeffrey said sadly, "I guess there aren't any clues here."

"Put the things back then," suggested Violet.

Just as Sammy was putting the pillow down he looked at it and stopped. "We didn't see this before! Look, there are letters here on the pillowslip."

Everybody came over to look. In tiny cross-stitch embroidery there were two letters, W and C.

"The C must stand for Carver," Jeffrey guessed. "But what about the W?"

"Think!" said Benny. "Maybe the W stands for the little boy's first name. It could be Walter or William."

"Or Wally," said Sammy. "Come on, maybe we can find something else."

Violet and Jessie took out every drawer of the desk. They were all empty. Violet put her hand into the empty spaces for the drawers to see if she could find a secret drawer. But there was nothing to find.

Jessie was looking at the top of the desk. "Look at this—here are some letters carved on the desk with a knife. It isn't very plain. Let's see. Here is a W and this must be an I."

Violet looked too. "There are two L's and a Y," she said.

"WILLY!" everybody shouted at once.

"I bet the little boy was named Willy Carver," said Sammy. "That goes with the initials on the pillowslip."

Benny and Henry had looked all around the window and door but they had found nothing. They looked at the old toys and shook the red slippers. But they could not find any new clues.

Jessie said, "Come on, Violet. Let's put the drawers back in the desk. Too bad it's all empty."

The big rocking horse stood in the center of the

room. Sammy patted its head. He ran his hand over its mane. He touched the saddle.

"Look," he called. "I think the saddle comes off. Help me undo this buckle."

Everyone gathered around. Violet unfastened the buckle. Benny helped Jeffrey lift the saddle. As the boys did so, something slipped from the rocking horse's back and fell to the floor.

Sammy crawled between the rockers and lifted the paper carefully. He handed it to Jessie. "You take it, Jessie," he said. "I'm afraid I'll tear it."

"I'm almost afraid to touch it myself," said Jessie. She took the folded paper. "It's a little book," she said. "Only four pages long."

The old paper was folded twice and pinned with a rusty pin to make a little book.

Sammy said, "Somebody drew a picture of the rocking horse on the cover."

Sure enough, there was a picture of the horse. It showed a little boy sitting on its back. Underneath was printed "My Pony."

Jessie turned the pages carefully. "It looks as if somebody wrote a story," she said.

"Read it," Sammy begged.

"Yes, read it," they all said.

The writing was faded and hard to read. Jessie read slowly.

" 'This is a true story,' " she began. " 'It is Willy's favorite story. Once upon a time there was a little boy named Willy. Every summer he came to Grandma Carver's house. Grandma loved Willy. She made a little room just for him up under the roof. Willy likes his little room.' "

Violet said, "Oh, Jessie, somebody must have written all that down for Willy. Maybe he liked to hear it at bedtime. Go on."

Jessie read on. " 'Willy has special toys at Grandma's. The most special of all is a rocking horse. It has been in Grandma's family for years and years. Many little boys have ridden it. Now Willy loves to ride it. He calls it his pony. The End.' "

"That's all?" Jeffrey asked.

"Yes," replied Jessie. "That's the end."

"We have two real clues," Benny said. "We know the little boy's name. And we know he came to visit his grandmother here. He didn't live here all the time. But why do you suppose the room was all closed up?"

"Well, that's still a mystery," said Henry.

Benny looked over at the toys he and Henry had found. He looked at the ball, the toy horn, and the little train engine. Suddenly something made him stand still.

"Wait," Benny said. "I'm getting some sort of idea. That horn reminds me of something."

Everyone stared at Benny. Nobody laughed. Then Benny smiled. "I know! Do you remember when we made the casserole?" he asked.

"Yes," Jessie said. "But what has that to do with this room?"

"Mrs. McGregor!" Benny said. "That's what! She told us when she was a little girl she came to this house for a birthday party. She remembered something about a toy horn and a little boy."

"It must have been Willy Carver's party!" Violet exclaimed. "If we tell her about this, maybe she can remember something more."

"Come on," Benny said. "Let's show her the horn and see."

Mrs. McGregor was in the kitchen. She dusted

flour off her hands and smiled at her visitors. She listened to their story and picked up the old toy horn.

"Oh, deary me!" she said. "How well I remember this little tin horn! The little boy had it for a birthday present. The boy in the sailor suit."

"That's good!" said Benny. "That's a good clue, Mrs. McGregor."

Mrs. McGregor still held the little tin horn in her hands. She said, "I wish I could tell you more."

"You have told us a lot," said Violet. "Maybe if we knew when the party was it might help. At least we would know when the room was still open."

"That's right," agreed Henry.

Mrs. McGregor thought for a minute. "Let me see. It was before we moved to the farm. I was five then. So the party must have been when I was about four years old. That would be 1910. Yes, it must have been the summer of 1910. I'm sure it was summer. I had a sunbonnet."

"A name and a date," Benny said. "That ought to help us. But I don't know how yet."

Mrs. McGregor said, "I'm afraid that's all I can do. I wish I knew someone else who might remember the Carvers. They were important people in Greenfield, but they have all been gone a long, long time."

"Let's go up in the tree house and think," Sammy said. "You come, too, Benny."

So Benny went back with Sammy and Jeffrey. By and by Mrs. Beach saw the boys up in the tree house.

"What's the matter?" she asked.

"We're thinking," Sammy said. "But we're not thinking."

Jeffrey explained, "We have some clues, but now we don't know what to do with them. We just can't think why that room was closed off."

"Tell me what you know so far," Mrs. Beach suggested.

The boys told her they knew it was Willy Carver's room and that he had visited his grandmother in the summer of 1910.

"But that's so long ago no one can remember anything," Jeffrey said.

"There aren't any Carvers left in Greenfield," Benny said.

Mrs. Beach said, "That doesn't mean you have to stop hunting. I have been writing a book about people who came to America in 1685. I have been able to find out a lot about them. You just have to know where to look."

"Look?" said Benny. Then suddenly he guessed what Mrs. Beach meant. "I know!" he exclaimed. "The library!"

CHAPTER 9

Good News

It was library day when Violet and Benny rode their bikes over to the Beaches. Jessie and Henry had made other plans and could not go, but Sammy and Jeffrey were waiting. They had notebooks and pencils.

"Follow us," Benny called. "We know the way."

Soon the four children were chaining their bicycles in front of the Greenfield Public Library. It was a large library for a small town.

Mrs. White was always glad to see the Aldens coming. She laughed. She said, "I know what you want, Benny. Some science books and some mystery books. And how about your new friends? Do they like mysteries?"

"Yes, but—" Sammy and Jeffrey both began at once. Then Jeffrey went on, "We have a real mystery story already. That's why we came."

Then Benny told Mrs. White about the mystery room. He said, "We want to know one special thing. Why was the room closed up?"

"What a puzzle!" Mrs. White exclaimed. "I hope I can help you find out. I won't promise. You are lucky to have that date, 1910. Come with me and I'll show you what we have. You may find some clues."

Mrs. White led the children into a room in another part of the library. "People often come to learn about past times in Greenfield. We keep everything about Greenfield history here," she said. "We have some interesting things like old letters people have given to the library. There are old books and newspapers, too. Now let's see. Where shall we begin?"

Violet said, "We thought maybe old copies of the Greenfield News might help us. The Carvers had that big house and were an important family."

"A good place to begin," Mrs. White agreed. "We

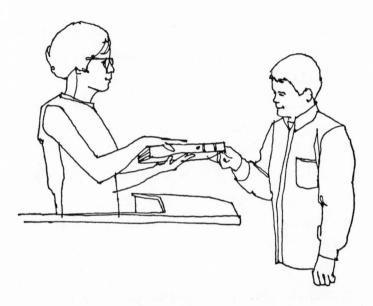

have the old newspapers made into big books. Sit down at this long table and I will bring you some. You can begin with June, July, and August of 1910."

Soon Mrs. White put the big books on the table. She looked at Sammy and asked, "Do you think you can read these newspapers? They are not easy."

Jeffrey said, "Sammy can read anything." And Mrs. White was surprised to find out later that this was true.

After the librarian had gone, the room was very still. The Aldens and the Beaches were busy looking at the old copies of the Greenfield News.

"Here," Sammy whispered. "Look at this—there's a story on the front page about this library. It was first opened on June 5, 1910."

"Here's something about a big fire," Benny said. "A lumberyard burned. It says it was once owned by the Carver family. I guess they were important people."

"I'm going to look on the pages that tell about neighbors visiting and having parties," Violet said. "I think that's where we might see something about Willy's grandmother."

Jeffrey and Sammy looked through several papers but they did not find anything.

Suddenly Violet whispered, "Here! It says something about Mrs. A. M. Carver. Oh, it's just about a meeting of church ladies. That doesn't help us."

The children began to feel tired. The print in the old newspapers was small and hard to read. It wasn't as easy as they had hoped. But nobody wanted to give up.

Mrs. White looked in. "Any luck?" she asked.

Just then Jeffrey began to breathe hard. He said, "Listen. Here it is." Then he read a notice. It said, "Mrs. A. M. Carver is entertaining her grandson Willy for the summer. He is the son of Joseph Carver of London, England, who is in the coal mining business there. Willy will return to his parents on August first of this year."

"Oh, good for you!" said Violet. "You found the first good clue, Jeff."

Benny had the July papers and now he said, "Here's a little story about Willy's birthday party. Certainly that's the one Mrs. McGregor remembers."

Sammy said, "Let's see if there is a story about Willy going home. Look in the August newspapers."

All four children looked, trying to read as fast as they could.

It was Benny who found what they wanted. He read, " 'This week Mr. and Mrs. Joseph Carver came to Greenfield to get their son and take him back to England. They are returning to live in London permanently, taking Mrs. A. M. Carver with them. The Carver family home has been rented to Mr. and Mrs. David Johnson, who will occupy it the first of September. The Johnsons have five children.' "

"Now that's something new!" Benny said. "We didn't know anyone lived in the house between the Carvers and the first Beach family."

"And now we have the Johnsons," agreed Violet.

"With five kids," added Jeffrey.

All at once Sammy said, "Now everyone keep still and let me think! I have an idea and then I lose it. Here it is again. Suppose Mrs. Carver didn't want five strange children playing with all Willy's toys. I'll bet she closed up that room and hid it so that nobody would know it was there."

Benny said slowly, "You may be right, Sammy. At least nobody ever found it until we did. I haven't any better ideas."

Violet said, "I don't think we can find anything

more here. Nobody would put anything about that closed room in the newspapers. It was such a secret."

"Let's show that nice librarian what we found," Sammy said. "I copied it in my notebook."

Mrs. White was glad to hear what the children had found. "Do come again," she said. "You read very well, Sammy."

"I'll come again," Sammy said. "I want a book about the moon's surface."

"We have many of those," said Mrs. White with a smile. "I'll try to pick out a hard one for you."

Violet, Benny, Jeffrey, and Sam started home on their bikes. Sammy said, "We've been so excited about the mystery room that we haven't finished the tree house."

"We can finish it after lunch," Jeff said.

Benny said, "You can put up the lantern and the mailbox and the rope ladder."

Later that afternoon Sammy said, "I wish Dad and Mom would come home. I want to tell them what we found in the library."

Jeffrey said, "I've been thinking about Uncle Max. He might remember something more if we told him about the Johnsons and their five children. I'd like to know if Sammy's idea is right."

When Mr. and Mrs. Beach came home, they found the tree house done and the backyard picked up.

"Didn't you go to the library after all?" asked Mrs. Beach. "Come in and tell me."

They all went into the living room and the children sat down on the floor.

"Oh, we went all right, Mom!" said Sammy. "And just listen to this. We found it in the old newspapers." He took out his notebook and read his notes to his parents.

Mr. Beach said, "I never heard of the Johnsons. I wonder if Max has. Maybe he has forgotten them, too. Would you like to drive over there this evening after dinner and ask him?"

Jeffrey said, "Oh, Dad, that is the very thing we want most."

Sammy was very quiet. He was thinking. All at

once he exclaimed, "I have the most stupendous idea! Uncle Max could name his restaurant the Rocking Horse! We could give him the big rocking horse for children to look at. They couldn't ride on it because it is so old. But children would want to come and so their parents would bring them, and the eating place would be a great success."

Benny said, "That's the best idea yet. I would want to go to a place named the Rocking Horse."

"So would I," said Mrs. Beach.

But Jeffrey was thinking, too. He said, "Dad, do the toys in the hidden room belong to us?"

"Yes, they do," replied his father. "I bought the house and everything in it and the land around it. So if you want to give the toys to Uncle Max, you may. Of course Uncle Max may not like the idea."

"I think he will, Mr. Beach," said Benny. "He is ready to try almost anything."

Violet said, "We have to go. It's dinner time."

Mrs. Beach said, "Come back later and drive to Uncle Max's with us. It's everybody's mystery now."

CHAPTER 10

An Old Secret

Uncle Max was glad to see his brother's family coming to visit. Benny had come along, too.

"You see I have started to cut a long window," Max said, pointing at the front wall of the restaurant. "This place is already a lot lighter."

"The boys have a question they want to ask you, Max," said Mrs. Beach.

"I hope I can answer it," he said.

Sammy told about the newspaper stories about Willy Carver, Mrs. Carver, and the Johnsons. Before he had finished, Uncle Max began to nod his head.

"Yes," he said, "our father bought the house from Joseph Carver, but I remember it had to be all cleaned up because so many children had lived there. Don't you recall, John? No, I guess you were too little to notice."

"I guess I was," Mr. Beach said.

"Then there was something else," Uncle Max said and frowned. "I can't think. It was a visitor. I was only a kid myself."

"Oh, think hard," begged Sammy. "Was the visitor a man or a woman?"

"It was a man," answered Uncle Max. "A young man. He came to see our father. He spoke in a way that seemed funny to me. You know, he said 'rawther' for 'rather'."

"That sounds English," Mrs. Beach said.

"Well," Uncle Max went on, "my dad and the young man went upstairs and all over the house. They were looking for something, but I don't know what it was. I am sure they did not find anything because the young man was disappointed when he left."

"Did they go up to the third floor?" Benny asked.

"Yes, I remember climbing the stairs behind them."

Jeffrey looked ready to burst with an idea. He said, "I can guess who that was. It must have been Willy Carver. He would have been grown-up then and maybe he wanted to find his old room."

Benny said, "I think you're right, Jeff. I'm sure he never forgot that big rocking horse."

Sammy said, "He'd never guess part of his old room had been closed off and the door covered with wallpaper. He must have thought the toys and rocking horse were lost or taken away by someone else."

"It does all fit in," said Uncle Max. "Quite a mystery. If his grandmother closed that room off, she never told him about it."

"And now let's talk about your restaurant," said John Beach.

Max shook his head. "I haven't thought of a good name for it yet."

Sammy could not wait. "I have! It's the most stupendous name—the Rocking Horse!"

Uncle Max burst out laughing. "It is a stupendous name, Sammy. How did you ever think of it?"

"Well, you know that rocking horse that belonged to Willy? We could bring it down and put it beside the door and then put all the other old toys on shelves around the room for children to look at."

Mrs. Beach said, "I think everyone would like to see those toys. They are so old and interesting."

"We must have a sign outside!" cried Uncle Max. "I can make it myself just exactly like the old rocking horse. I'll have to see it first."

"Right," said his brother. "I know you like to draw. Come and have dinner with us tomorrow and see the toys."

Uncle Max winked at Sammy. "I'd like to eat in the tree house," he said.

"Let's make it a backyard dinner," Mr. Beach said.

"And invite the Aldens," Jeffrey said.

"That would make ten," said Sammy instantly.

"I'll come and bring two apple pies," agreed Uncle Max.

"Oh, good!" said Benny. "You make the best apple pie I ever ate—except that one Jessie made using a glass bottle for a rolling pin."

When the Aldens came over to the backyard of the Beach house the next evening they were surprised. Mr. Beach had brought out a charcoal stove.

"I didn't know you could cook, Dad!" said Jeffrey.

"I think I can cook hamburger," his father said.

A few minutes later Uncle Max came into the yard. He was carrying two apple pies and a small package wrapped in brown paper. Henry took one pie and Jessie took the other, but Uncle Max kept the package. He said hello to everyone, then he looked up at the tree house. He walked all around it.

"That's a good tree house, boys," he said. "It is better than ours. And where is that round window?"

"You can't see it from the ground," said Jeffrey. "Climb up into the tree and we'll show you. You are going to eat dinner up here with us, you know."

The two boys had climbed the rope ladder, but Uncle Max went up the ladder. Henry had made a

wooden cover for the knothole. Jeffrey opened it and took out the telescope and gave it to his uncle. "See," he said, "look under the roof. Right over there."

"There it is!" said Uncle Max. "You're right!"

When dinner was ready, Sammy and Jeffrey let down the basket and Jessie put in paper plates with hamburgers, and pickles. There was milk for the boys and coffee for Uncle Max. Later there was pie and cheese.

After dinner it was time to show Uncle Max the attic. Jeffrey and Sammy started off with him when Mr. Alden surprised them by getting up. "I'd like to go, too," he said.

The boys showed Uncle Max the wallpaper, the round window, and all the toys. They showed him the rocking horse.

Uncle Max took a tape measure out of his pocket. He measured the horse and rockers. He looked carefully at the colors. Then he drew a picture of the horse on a sketch pad he had brought.

"I see how well you draw," Mr. Alden said. "That

will be a fine sign. I'd like to help the new restaurant in some way. Why don't you buy what you need for the sign and send the bill to me?"

Uncle Max agreed because he knew that Mr. Alden really was interested in the restaurant.

When everyone was in the yard again and it was almost time to go Uncle Max said, "I've been thinking about the mystery of the closed room. I thought I did not have any clues, but perhaps I am wrong."

Now Uncle Max took the package that he had brought. He took off the brown paper and held out a leather-covered book. There were words in gold letters on the cover. They said "Household Journal."

Everyone waited for Uncle Max to explain.

"When we moved away from this house," he said, "we packed our books into boxes. I did not have any reason to look at the books that belonged to me for a long time. When I did, I found that this book had been packed with mine. It never belonged to me, so it must have been a mistake."

Uncle Max opened the book and everyone saw that

about half of it was filled with handwritten notes. In fact, it looked like a diary with dates written in it.

"To tell the truth," Uncle Max said, "I thought I might tear out these pages and use the rest of the book for sketching. But I never did, and I just kept the book. It wasn't my father's book, and I decided it must have been left in the house at one time and mixed in with our books."

Sammy couldn't wait any longer. "But what does it say?" he asked.

Uncle Max said, "I knew you'd ask. I have been reading it, and now I think that this belonged to Mrs. Carver, Willy's grandmother. She wrote down people who came to visit, things she ordered for the house, and the vegetables in her own garden."

The children didn't see how that would help solve the mystery but they waited.

"Look here," Uncle Max said. "Here is a page dated April 5, 1910. It shows that Mrs. Carver bought five rolls of wallpaper. 'For little W's room,' it says."

Jessie said, "That's the paper with the drums and toys used for the closet and Willy's room! She was getting ready for his visit."

Uncle Max turned the page. "For July 10 it says 'W's birthday. Ordered cake and favors for ten children.'"

"That's right!" Sammy said. "We read about the party in the old newspaper at the library. It's the one Mrs. McGregor remembers."

"Now," said Uncle Max, "see if you can read this last page for yourselves."

The date was August 15, 1910. The writing was faded and hard to read. It was Jessie who puzzled it out. This is what she read: "House rented to Johnson family. Cannot bear to think of strange children playing with W's toys. Finished papering closet before packing to leave. Hope to return next year."

For a minute everyone was quiet. Then Benny said, "That makes our guess right. Mrs. Carver closed up the room herself."

"She never told anyone," Henry said. "She

thought she was coming back. But we know that she didn't."

"And so the rocking horse has been hidden all this time!" said Jeffrey. "I'm glad we're the ones who found it."

Uncle Max said, "I am, too. And now the rocking horse will have a new home and lots and lots of children will see it—I hope."

CHAPTER 11

Lost and Found

There was plenty to do to help Uncle Max get his restaurant open.

Jessie and Violet made bright yellow curtains for the big new window. Jeffrey and Sam wrote a story about the rocking horse. Mr. Alden had it printed on place mats with a picture of the rocking horse in the middle. Henry and Benny helped paint and make shelves to hold the old toys. Uncle Max put up his new sign outside.

The Rocking Horse Restaurant was to have its big opening day on a Saturday. There was an advertisement in the Greenfield News. On Friday Henry, the other Aldens, with Jeffrey and Sammy, took the old toys to Uncle Max. Jessie and Violet had flowers to put on the tables.

Jeffrey and Sammy carried Willy Carver's wonderful old rocking horse from the Alden station wagon. Soon the horse was standing in its special place just inside the door at one side. Children coming in could see it and pat its nose but they could not ride it. That would have been too much for the old horse.

On opening day the restaurant was clean and shining. The new window let in the sunlight. Uncle Max had bought more tables and chairs. The new sign hung outside on an iron pole. Place mats were on the tables, and everything was ready.

The Aldens and the Beaches came before noon. Everyone was almost too excited to do anything. But they helped Uncle Max in every way they could. Jessie and Violet set the tables. Benny and the Beach boys peeled potatoes.

"You are certainly a lot of help to me," said Uncle Max. "What should I do without you?"

Sammy said, "I guess you think we act as if the

Rocking Horse Restaurant is ours. Anyway we can't stay away."

Jessie said, "I almost wish we weren't going on our vacation so soon. We are leaving next week."

"I'm sorry," said Uncle Max. "I didn't know you Aldens were going away so soon."

But Sammy said, "We'll be here, Uncle Max."

Jeffrey added, "We'll keep you company. We'll come to lunch and dinner often."

Everything was ready now. There was nothing to do but wait. At eleven o'clock no customers had come. Everyone was afraid there wouldn't be any customers at all.

But at half-past eleven they changed their minds. They were afraid there would be too many customers! More and more people kept coming in.

Many children came. They loved the rocking horse and the story on the place mats. And they liked Uncle Max's cooking, too. They begged their parents to bring them again.

When all the customers had gone, the Aldens and

the Beaches sat down to talk over the day. What a success it had been!

John Beach said, "Of course this was your biggest day. It won't be like this every day."

"I hope not," said Uncle Max. "I like to wait on the children myself. I like to hear them talk. It will be fine if the restaurant is just busy enough for me to do all the work."

"Well, you heard them today," said Benny. "The children certainly had a good time. They'll be back."

Suddenly Uncle Max began to laugh. He said, "I almost forgot. Now that we are alone, I have a surprise for everybody. Excuse me a minute."

Uncle Max went behind the counter and came out carrying an enormous cake.

"Just look at that cake!" exclaimed Jessie. "Did you make it, Uncle Max?"

"I did," said Uncle Max. "I wanted to say thank you to everybody."

Max had done his best. The frosting was creamy white, decorated with pink roses and pale green leaves. In the middle of the cake was a beautiful rocking horse made of frosting.

"Oh, it's too pretty to cut!" said Violet.

The cake was as good as it looked. It was soon cut and everyone began to eat. It was a wonderful way for Uncle Max to say thank you.

As Sammy finished his large piece, he said, "I want to tell you something, Benny."

"Go right ahead," said Benny. "I'm listening."

"I want to thank you for everything," said Sammy. "I didn't know how to pull out a nail, and I couldn't climb. I didn't know how to make things, and I didn't even know how to make friends. Now I can make friends with anybody."

The others listened. They knew it was true.

But Benny said, "Now you listen, Sammy. Thank you for all you taught me."

"I taught you?" cried Sammy. "I couldn't teach you anything!"

"Oh, yes, you did, Sammy. I learned from you and Jeffrey that sometimes I ought to shut my mouth and stop talking—and think. So that's what I'm going to do."

"Oh, don't, Ben!" said Jessie. "You wouldn't be Benny any more if you didn't talk all the time."

"I'll *think* about it anyway," said Benny.

Everybody laughed.

Then Jeffrey said, "I've been thinking, too, and I think we ought to thank the Aldens for the tree house. If they hadn't helped us build the tree house, none of this would have happened."

"That's right, Jeff," said Sammy. "We would never have found the spyglass."

"We would never have found the little round window," added Jeffrey.

"You would never have found the rocking horse," said Mrs. Beach.

"There wouldn't have been a Rocking Horse Restaurant," said Mr. Beach.

Uncle Max nodded his head. "A lot of things have been lost and found: the spyglass, the rocking horse, a whole room—and a brother." He looked at John

Beach. "Without the tree house, I don't think I would have found my brother quite so soon. Do you, John?"

"I have to agree, Max, and I'm glad we are good friends at last." He shook hands with Max.

When it was time to go home, Mrs. Beach took Jessie and Violet by the hand. She smiled at them, but she said nothing.

Mr. Beach went out with Mr. Alden. He said, "After this, our family is going to have fun together. Just the way you do. We have found that our boys mean more to us than anything else in the whole world."

"Good," said Grandfather. "I'm glad. I had to learn that the hard way a long time ago." And as he said this he thought about how his grandchildren had once made a home for themselves in an old boxcar.

As Henry drove home, Benny said, "We had a lot of fun. But the best part about the whole thing is Mr. Beach and Uncle Max being friends again."

And everyone agreed with Benny.

GERTRUDE CHANDLER WARNER discovered when she was teaching that many readers who like an exciting story could find no books that were both easy and fun to read. She decided to try to meet this need, and her first book, *The Boxcar Children*, quickly proved she had succeeded.

Miss Warner drew on her own experiences to write the mystery. As a child she spent hours watching trains go by on the tracks opposite her family home. She often dreamed about what it would be like to set up housekeeping in a caboose or freight car—the situation the Alden children find themselves in.

When Miss Warner received requests for more adventures involving Henry, Jessie, Violet, and Benny Alden, she began additional stories. In each, she chose a special setting and introduced unusual or eccentric characters who liked the unpredictable.

While the mystery element is central to each of Miss Warner's books, she never thought of them as strictly juvenile mysteries. She liked to stress the Aldens' independence and resourcefulness and their solid New England devotion to using up and making do. The Aldens go about most of their adventures with as little adult supervision as possible—something else that delights young readers.

Miss Warner lived in Putnam, Connecticut, until her death in 1979. During her lifetime, she received hundreds of letters from girls and boys telling her how much they liked her books. And so she continued the Aldens' adventures, writing a total of nineteen books in the Boxcar Children series.